Tall Pine Mystery

Tall Pine Mystery

WRITTEN BY
NAN DOERKSEN

OMF
INTERNATIONAL

TALL PINE MYSTERY
Copyright © 2002 Nan Doerksen
ISBN: 0-9731833-0-6
Printed in Canada by *Essence Publishing*.
Published by OMF International, 5155 Spectrum Way, Building 21, Mississauga, ON L4W 5A1, Canada.

OMF Books are distributed by:
OMF, 5155 Spectrum Way, Bldg. 21, Mississauga, ON L4W 5A1, Canada
OMF, 10 West Dry Creek Circle, Littleton, CO 80120, U.S.A.
OMF, Station Approach, Borough Green, Sevenoaks, Kent TN15 8BG, United Kingdom
OMF, PO Box 849, Epping, NSW 1710, Australia
OMF, PO Box 10–159, Auckland, 1030, New Zealand
OMF, PO Box 3080, Pinegowrie 2123, South Africa
and other OMF offices

Cover art and inside illustrations created by Sylvia Draaistra

Table of Contents

Chapter One

Counting Water Buffaloes

KIMBERLY ANN was up and dressed, ready to go, before her sister Sandra Louise was awake. Only her brown, curly hair showed as she slept, facing the wall. Too excited to sleep, Kim had awakened even before the birds started to sing. Dad had told them to be ready by seven o'clock when he would be there with the Land-Rover, to take them home for the Christmas holiday. Already it was past six-thirty. Impatiently, Kim tugged at the blanket.

"Sandee! Sandee! Wake up and hurry. Dad will be here any minute and we have to have breakfast before we go. Get up!"

Abruptly, Sandee pushed back her blanket and sat up, blinking. Without a word, she jumped out of bed and got

7

dressed in a flash. Together they dashed downstairs to the kitchen where Auntie Jean, the house-mother of River House, the boarding home for OMF International children, was preparing their breakfast.

"Special treat today," she said, smiling. "Mango juice and pancakes." She watched as they filled their plates, asked a blessing on their food, and began eating rapidly. "You don't have to rush, you know," she said. "Your Dad might be hungry too. And here he is now," she added, glancing out the window. But he had already eaten, "ages ago," he said, so he only drank a glass of mango juice and then went to fetch the girls' suitcases while they finished eating.

Malcolm and Susan Green, with their two daughters, had come to Thailand from Fredericton, New Brunswick in Canada, to work for OMF International. At first the whole family had stayed together while they learned to speak the Thai language and got used to the way people lived there. Sandee and Kim, as everyone called them, who were ten and eight years old now, went to an English school, but they learned to speak Thai, too, much faster than their parents. Four months earlier, Mom and Dad had moved to a new village of Pwo Karen tribes-people, called Tall Pine Village, not too far from other mission stations at Striped Creek and Prosperity Fields. Because there was no school in the village, the girls stayed at River House, with other children, in the city of Chiang Mai. This would be their first visit to their new home.

"Okay girls, finish up," Dad said, coming into the kitchen again. "We have a long ride ahead of us and I have all kinds of food from the market to get home before it spoils, so let's get on the road before it's too hot. Ready?"

The inside of the Land-Rover was already warm as the girls slid in among the parcels, with Sandee in the front and Kim in the back. They could tell Dad was excited too, by the way he squealed the tires when they started out, as they waved goodbye to Auntie Jean. The streets were busy with buses, cars, and bicycles weaving in and out, and, sometimes, people dashing quickly across. Dad had to concentrate on driving. Once a 'songtow', a little truck used as a bus, filled with people, pulled past the Rover and squeezed directly in front of it, making Dad slam on his brakes to avoid an accident. They were all glad when they were outside the city on highway number eight, heading south towards Hod.

"How long will it take to get to Tall Pine Village, Dad?" Sandee asked. "Will we be there by lunch-time? Did you bring lunch?"

"We'll stop in Hod to have something to eat; it's the last good stopping place before our turn-off. After that the roads are not very good, especially once we get on the last mountainous stretch past Striped Creek. There's only a very rough road up to our village; that's why Mom didn't come along—too bumpy." He glanced back at Kim in the rear-view mirror. "You do remember, don't you, that you'll be having a baby sister or brother in the New Year?"

"Of course," both girls said at once.

"It had better be a brother," added Sandee. "One younger sister is enough; it's time we had a boy, or any baby; we're getting to be so old."

Dad laughed. "Either will be fine with Mom and me; we think girls are pretty good, really, even after knowing you two for such a long time. Hey, it's going to be great to have you home for the next month! Every time something new happens we say 'I wish the girls were here to see this, or taste this or do this job for us!' We have missed you very much. Life in Tall Pine Village is different from life in Chiang Mai, but you'll love it."

Traffic continued to be heavy, mostly with buses and trucks. There were rice fields on both sides of the road and, since it was harvest time, there were people and water-buffaloes working in the fields. Nearby were little villages with low, wooden houses surrounded by fruit trees and gardens and pens with pigs and chickens. Once in a while they could see a church, but more often, there was a yellow Buddhist temple, or Wat, as the Thai people call it. Away beyond the rice fields, there were mountains, greenly covered with bamboo, teak and even pine trees.

"I counted nine water-buffaloes in that last lot of fields we passed," Sandee announced suddenly. "What did you count, Kim?"

"I was looking for horses, the way we used to on drives back home and we said, 'zip', every time we saw one, but there haven't been any."

"We could try it on bicycles," suggested Sandee. "There are enough of those, or people in the fields? No, too many. Maybe people dressed in red only, or white."

"Red," said Kim. "Too many in white."

Time passed so quickly as they concentrated on what was happening outside the car that the girls were surprised when Dad said, "There's Hod up ahead. We'll stop at a restaurant for something to eat."

Sandee and Kim were hungry. Dad ordered noodles for all of them, with soft drinks for the girls and tea for himself. Each of them was given a bowl with a spoon and chopsticks; then a large plate of spicy noodles with red peppers, chopped vegetables, and little pieces of pork was placed in the centre of the table. All of them were good at using chopsticks by now and they finished the noodles quickly.

"Before we leave Hod," Dad said, "I want to buy a Christmas surprise for your mother in the craft shops. Can you keep a secret? If you won't tell Mom what I buy, you can help me select it."

They went to a craft shop which specialized in silver necklaces made by the Pwo Karen. There were many beautiful ones from which to choose, but it took a while—after they had looked at every one—to agree on which one was the best. Dad tucked it carefully inside his backpack.

The time on the road from Hod to the Striped Creek turn-off went by quickly—both girls were feeling hot and sleepy. They kept dozing off, forgetting to count water-buffaloes or anything else. Suddenly the road became very bumpy, as Dad shifted into low gear and slowed way down. Sandee sat up, brushing her hair off her damp forehead, wide awake now. The road was only a narrow trail really, climbing up towards the mountains, circling around large rocks, through bushes and trees, including newly planted pine trees.

"Won't be much longer now," Dad said, glancing quickly at Sandee's flushed face. "Have a drink from the water bottle; you look very hot. Better wake up Kim too; she won't want to miss this."

Kim sat up quickly when Sandee reached back to give her a shake, her red hair wet with sweat and the sprinkle of freckles across her nose showing brightly. She took a few minutes to wake fully, then gazed out the window at the strange wilderness around them. Some large birds were circling overhead and, once, some startled deer bounded off, making barking sounds. When they came to the top of a steep hill, Dad stopped the Rover, which had been struggling, to give it a rest and to let the girls see the spectacular view of hills and mountains spread out before them. Looking downward, they could see wisps of smoke rising in the distance.

"There it is," Dad pointed. "That's Tall Pine Village."

Kim and Sandee stared hard for a minute, but all they could see was forest.

"Are you sure Mom is down there?" Kim asked.

Dad looked surprised. "Yes, of course I'm sure."

"Then we'd better hurry down; she'll be awfully lonesome all by herself."

"You know you're probably right," Dad said. "Rover, are you ready?" He got out of the car to see how hot it was, then started the motor and drove carefully down the winding, rutty trail.

Tall Pine Village was small, only a dozen or so houses clustered together, but not too close, in a clearing hacked out of the forest. More or less in the centre of the village, stood a very tall, old pine, towering over the other trees. The houses all looked the same: made of wood, raised about a meter off the ground and on stilts. They were all single-story houses, some larger than others, but each with a verandah at the front or running right around the house; these had a low wall around them, and a ladder to climb onto the verandah. The roof was made of bamboo strips with large leaves fastened onto the bamboo, which made the houses feel very airy and cool in hot weather. Underneath the house there was room to shelter pigs and chickens, or for storage of tools and other things.

Dad turned in at the very first house they came to, a short distance off the road, at the edge of the village. Before the car even stopped, Mom was out on the verandah, waving at them. She waited for Sandee and Kim to climb up the ladder leading to the verandah; they rushed up and both hugged her at once. Surprised to see tears running down her face at the same time that she was laughing, Kim said, "Mom, don't cry now; we're here!"

"I know," Mom told them, "I'm so happy to see you. I've been waiting and waiting. But now we'd better help Dad bring in all the packages, and you can explore the house."

There wasn't much to explore. The house had four rooms—a large front room used for visiting, eating, and cooking, with a storage room off to one side. There were two bedrooms directly behind the front room, with curtains for doors, separated from each other with walls made of woven bamboo mats. Each bedroom had a screened window with shutters that could be closed at night. On the wooden floor were more mats. There was a bamboo bed with a thin mattress for each of the girls and some shelves for their clothes and other things. Both of the beds had mosquito nets, like tents, over them.

In the front room, there was a gas stove to cook on and a fire-box, sort of like an outdoor campfire, in the floor for heating the house on cold days, or for cooking. There was a table and chairs, but also mats to sit on, which the village people preferred. The whole house was very clean and airy.

"It's like a playhouse," Sandee called to her parents who were putting groceries away in the storage room. " A bit like the one Grandpa built for us when we were little, remember? What fun! But where's the bathroom?"

"Outside. Go look behind the house; there's a little building there. Wait, I'll go with you," Mom said. "You have to always check for snakes. I'll show you how to use it."

The girls went out onto the verandah, which was partially covered, and had a low wooden wall around it. Their parents had planted a garden on one side, including bougainvillaea and other flowering shrubs and fruit trees, still too young to bear fruit. They could see and hear chickens, fenced in, with a shelter under the house. A black cat came up the ladder onto the verandah and stared at the girls.

"Dad, there's a cat here!" Kim, who saw it first, called to him as he finished taking things out of the Land-Rover. "Is it ours?"

"Yes, that's one of our cats; we have two. That black one is Jasper," he said, coming up the ladder, "the other one, which is a female, is called Amber because she's mostly yellow. They are both very good mousers and snake catchers."

"Where did you get them?" Sandee wondered as she tried to stroke Jasper, who didn't seem to know whether to be friendly or not.

"Give him time, Sandee," Mom said, looking out at them. "They have to get used to children. There are lots of cats in the village; one of the families gave them to us.

They were kittens when we got them, so they're still pretty young. Supper's ready," she added. "Wash your hands really well and then we'll eat."

The Green family was still eating supper, the girls, sometimes both talking at once, happily telling about life in River House and school, when curious visitors began to arrive on their porch. Word had spread that the teacher's children had returned home from school. The three children, who were the first to arrive, didn't say anything, only stood near the open door, looking and giggling. Soon two women came, greeting them with, "Are you home?" (Na oh lo ah?) At Malcolm's invitation, they came in, sat down on the mats and made comments about the girls, which Kim and Sandee could not understand. Mom introduced the girls to the women, who seemed especially interested in Sandee's curly hair and Kim's freckles.

"Can they understand the Karen language?" one of them asked, and shook her head in surprise when Susan explained that they couldn't.

"But they will learn quickly," Malcolm said, "if they can play with your children."

The women got up to leave, and Susan politely asked, "Are you going?"

"We are going back now," (Ja ma tie lo) they answered, calling the children to come, and all five of them left together.

After the supper dishes were cleaned up the Green family sat down in the front room for a Bible story and prayer, before going to bed. Jasper came into the room and curled up on Susan's lap.

"That reminds me," she said, "of a story I heard about

a missionary who worked with the Pwo Karen a long time ago. Every morning when she sat down to pray and read her Bible her cat came to sit on her lap. One day, she was teaching one of the village women about praying to Jesus. The woman seemed interested, but she said: 'I couldn't be a Christian and pray to Jesus.' When the missionary asked, 'Why not? she said 'because I don't have a cat.'"

The girls and Dad laughed, but Sandee wondered, "Is that a true story, Mom? Because at River House we were hearing true stories about the olden days when OMF people first came to Thailand, and in 'history' at school we had stories too, but sometimes the teacher said the stories were true and other times she wasn't sure."

"I like all kinds of stories," Kim interrupted, "true or not."

"Well," Dad said, "sometimes it doesn't matter too much if stories are true or not, but when we are teaching people about God it is very important that we teach what is true. And, when we teach in a language we don't know very well we can't always be sure people understand words exactly as we mean them. People here don't just listen to us, they watch us all the time too, to see how we live."

"We can speak Thai," Kim said, "but we don't know this language at all, so they'll just have to watch us, I guess."

"You'll learn very quickly, don't worry about that," Mom said. "And now it's time for bed. I'll tuck the netting in for you tonight."

Chapter Two

....

Elephants Bathing

"**T**OMORROW I'LL take you around the village to meet the people," Mom promised, as she and Dad made sure there were no bugs or snakes in the beds, and tucked the netting over the whole mattress, to keep out any mosquitoes that might sneak into the house. "Be sure to stay under the netting," Mom told them. "We don't want you getting malaria."

Since it was already dark and they had been up very early, both girls fell asleep at once. They didn't wake up till the sun shone through the cracks around the shuttered windows, and they could hear their rooster crowing. Far away other roosters were crowing too, and birds were calling. They could hear their parents talking in the front room.

"We're awake," Sandee called. "Can we come out of here now?"

Mom came into their room. "Of course, come out and get dressed quickly. You can go with Dad to fetch water from the village well."

After breakfast Mom, Sandee and Kim started off to see the rest of the village. The first house they came to belonged to Headman Tiger, the most important person in the village. "Sort of like a town mayor back home," their mother explained. "Before we could stay in this village we had to get permission from him, and he decided where we could build our house."

The Headman was not at home, but Mrs. Tiger was sitting on the front porch weaving some pretty red cloth with a pattern of other colours. She was pleased to see Susan and the girls. She told them that most of the people in the village had gone to the fields to finish harvesting rice, since this was a good day for it.

"You won't see many people at the houses," she said, "but you could go see them in the fields."

"Thank you," said Susan. "Perhaps we will see you and the others tomorrow when we have the Bible teaching and singing at our house."

"If they are finished harvesting they will come," said Mrs. Tiger, going back to her weaving.

It didn't take long to go to all the houses in the village, because only one other person was at home. Granny Smiles was sitting on a mat in her front room, rocking a baby wrapped in a blanket. She explained that her grandchild was sick with a fever and would not eat.

Susan, who was a nurse, examined the baby and asked

if she could come back with some medicine.

"Yes, do that," Granny said. "Come back quickly, before the others get back. That would be better."

"We'll go home now, girls," Susan said, leading the way.

Before they had gone very far they heard children's voices, and the same three children who had come to their house, appeared on the path in front of them. This time they came right over. Susan told Sandee and Kim that the girls were Mung and Dee, and their brother, who was the middle child, was called Gleck. Because Mom had to get the medicine for the baby, she couldn't stay to talk, so she told the girls they could follow more slowly.

The five children looked at each other. No one said anything for a few minutes. Then Gleck started turning cartwheels, and fell flat on the path. He jumped up laughing, his dark eyes shining with fun, and they all laughed and laughed till they were tired. Just then Susan came hurrying back with the medicine. She looked surprised to see them still there, and told Sandee and Kim to run on home now. Mung and Dee followed a short distance, but then they said something, waved, and ran off to catch up with Gleck.

"Do you think we can learn to speak their language, Sandee?" Kim wondered. "It might be easier to teach them ours."

"Not for them," said Sandee. "Anyway, I think they are fun to play with. I guess we can learn Pwo Karen just as well as the Thai language."

"And French and English," said Kim. "What did Dad say we'd be?"

"Multi-something," said Sandee.

"Multi-linguists," said Dad, suddenly there in front of them. "Come on, you multi-linguists, help me gather the eggs and get started on our lunch. Your Mom is busy. After lunch we'll go watch the rice-harvesting."

Father, Sandee and Kim walked along a path a short distance through the woods, down hill, to an open area in the valley, surrounded by mountains and forest, to find the rice fields. The valley was divided into separate fields for each family. Men and women and children, dressed in bright red or white clothing, and some in shorts and t-shirts, were working in the fields. Some of the men were cutting the rice stalks with sharp sickles, others were putting it out to dry in rows, while still others were already threshing their rice, beating it against a large piece of wood, resting on a grass mat, from which they collect-ed the kernels.

"This is their most important crop," Dad explained to the girls, as they watched from the edge of the fields. "They eat rice pretty well with every meal, so they need a lot of it, and they also want to sell some so that they have money to buy other things. The rice grown in Thailand is the best in the world."

Nobody really had time to stop and talk, though some of the people greeted them in a friendly way, but then went right on working. Some of the men did not seem friendly.

"Let's walk around the edge of the field," Dad sug-gested. "We don't want to get in their way."

As they came to the far side of one field, a man work-ing there noticed them, straightened up and came towards them quickly, speaking loudly, in an angry voice. Dad stopped the girls and spoke to the man. But the man would not listen; instead he seemed to be trying to chase them away.

"We'd better leave," Dad said to the girls. "He doesn't want us here."

Feeling frightened, the girls quickly turned back, with Dad following, after trying once more to be friendly.

When they were back on the path, Sandee asked Dad, "Who was that? Why was he angry at us?"

"It's strange, but I didn't recognize him," Dad said. "I thought I knew all the people here. I'll have to ask Headman Tiger about him. He certainly did not want us going near him."

"What was he saying, Dad?" Kim asked. "Could you understand him?"

"He just said, 'Go away—you can't come here.' He knew who we were, though, and if he has a field the other people must know him too. Strange."

Dad was thoughtful the rest of the way home. As they climbed up the hill the girls felt hot and tired. They were glad to get back to their cool, leafy-roofed porch, with Jasper and Amber coming to greet them. Mom was resting. Dad went in to get cold drinks from the refrigerator, and suggested Sandee and Kim find something quiet to do so as not to disturb her.

Sandee found a book to read while Kim continued to play with the cats. She found a dry leaf that had fallen from the roof, which made a rustling sound when dragged along the porch; the cats pounced and chased it, as she moved it around. Amber, tiring of the game, gave one more pounce, grabbed the leaf in her mouth and ran off the porch along the path to the well. Kim jumped down and ran after her. When Sandee looked up a minute later Kim was already out of sight.

Hadn't Dad told them not to go off alone, Sandee wondered? She looked into the front room, but Dad wasn't there; he must have gone for a rest too, Sandee decided. She got up and started down the path, calling her sister softly, so as not to disturb her parents. But, Kim was still out of sight. Sandee ran more quickly and soon came to the well. She stopped and listened. Something was making loud, splashing noises. Dad had said there was a creek down there, with a waterfall where they sometimes went to bathe. Could Kim have gone there?

"Kimberly!" Sandee called loudly, startling some parakeets into loud squawks, "come back here!"

In a minute Kim came running towards her, her face shining with excitement. "Quick, Sandee, come with me," she said, "there are elephants down there having a bath! Hurry!"

They both ran back to the creek, slowing down only as they reached the water, but keeping out of sight behind big trees. Two large elephants were having a glorious time hosing themselves down, snorting, grunting and splashing as they did so. Then they heaved themselves out of the water, on the side away from the girls, and lumbered off into the forest.

Sandee and Kim looked at each other with big grins on their faces; then Kim remembered she was chasing Amber and still hadn't found her.

"We'd better leave her now," Sandee told her. "Cats usually find their way home. Mom and Dad might be looking for us. Won't they be surprised when we tell them what we saw!"

"Elephants?" Dad said, opening his eyes very wide. "That's interesting. I know some of the Karen people use elephants to haul teak wood out to sell, but no one in this village has elephants. Some one from another village must be logging nearby. Did you see any men?"

"No, Dad, just elephants. But maybe somebody called them and that's why they left. Couldn't they be wild elephants?" asked Kim.

"There are not many wild elephants left in the mountains; most of them are owned by people," Dad explained. "Anyway, Sandee and Kim, you are not to go running off into the forest like this! There are snakes and tigers and who knows what around, and you are new to this place. You really must be more careful!"

That evening, as they were getting ready for bed, Sandee asked, "What happened to the baby, Mom? Do you think the medicine will make her well?"

"It will help. I also asked Granny Smiles if I could pray for the baby, and she was happy to have me do that. We can pray for her again now, and for the village people, that they will come to our church service tomorrow—and to the special Christmas celebration we will have here in two weeks time, when some of the Christian families from Striped Creek will come to celebrate with us."

"Only two weeks to Christmas!" said Kim. "Will there be presents and everything?"

Dad and Mom laughed. "There will be presents, but I don't know about 'everything', Kim, but it will be wonderful, you'll see," Dad told her.

"I was thinking about what you said yesterday, Sandee," Mom told her, "you know, stories about missionaries, and I remembered another one I heard. Two women working even farther north than this, were walking home one afternoon after visiting some of the Mien tribes-people. They were walking in a forest along a path for a long time, and at last, realized they were lost. It was beginning to get dark; they were not near any houses and did not meet any people they could ask. They decided to pray for help. A short while later, a Mien man, whom they had never seen before, came along the path and they asked him for directions. He showed them exactly where to go, and then left. They never saw him again, but were quite sure he must have been an angel sent by God in answer to their prayer! And yes, Sandee, this is a true story."

Chapter Three

Exploring the Village

DAD WAS up with the sunrise the next morning, cleaning up and getting things ready for the worship service at their house. Because he still did not know the Pwo Karen language well, he used tapes, made by Christians who did. There were music tapes with hymns and choruses, and teaching tapes which explained who Jesus was, why God sent him, how he died for our sins and came alive again to give us everlasting life. He had large posters that could be used to explain all this too.

At breakfast the whole Green family again prayed that the villagers would come to worship with them. Then Dad started playing a music tape, quite loudly, so that the village people would hear it. Sandee and Kim helped spread the mats and low benches around for people to sit on.

Amber and Jasper walked around inspecting everything, and the chickens under the house cackled and sang too.

It wasn't long before Mung and Dee arrived, giggling shyly as they sat down on a mat near the tape-player. Sandee and Kim sat down near them. Granny Smiles and her daughter, carrying the baby, came together, and several more children arrived running and out of breath. Only one other woman came.

Dad started the music tape over again, quieter this time, inviting everyone to sing along, which they tried to do, though they did not always get the tune exactly right. Sandee and Kim sang along in English. Then Mom told the story of the lost sheep and the good shepherd, using pictures, and trying to speak correct Pwo Karen. Amber came and curled up on Sandee's lap, purring loudly. One of their hens escaped from the pen and jumped onto the verandah. Several children, including Kim, got up and chased it back. Once or twice Granny Smiles corrected Mom's language, but she listened very closely. After that Dad put on another tape with a Bible reading and a short teaching on the reading, and then they sang the songs again.

"Help me get the cold tea to pass around, Sandee," Mom whispered to her, after Dad had prayed at the end of the singing.

The women stayed to talk and ask questions. The children began to play a game of tag and soon were told, by Granny Smiles, to run off and play somewhere else. The baby began to fuss and the women also got up and left.

"Why do the children have strings tied around their wrists?" Kim wondered, as soon as they were gone. "They all did, even the baby. They don't look very pretty."

"Well, they're not meant to look pretty," Dad explained. "It is something they do to protect their children from bad spirits; they believe it will keep them safe. Of course, we know that only Jesus can keep us safe from evil spirits and that is what we are trying to teach them. When they believe in Jesus they will cut off the strings and burn them." When he saw how surprised and serious Sandee and Kim looked, Dad gave them a big hug. "Things are very different here from Canada," he said. "The people in Tall Pine Village had not heard the good news about Jesus yet; that's why we came here—to tell them. And you can help too, by being friends with the children. Now, let's go see if our hen is back in the pen."

The next few days were very busy ones. The rice harvest was finished, with the rice stored away or being taken to the market. The Greens bought a supply of rice to store for the next months, since they did not have a field of their own.

Now, the people who were teaching their language to Mom and Dad, came again every day to spend several hours with them. Sandee and Kim sat for a little while to listen too, but soon tired of that. They were told they could go play with the other children, or near the house, but they were not to go into the forest beyond the well, without permission.

Every day now, Mung and Dee came to play with Sandee and Kim. Sometimes they played 'school', with Sandee as teacher, helping Mung and Dee to learn English, or teaching them other things she had learned in school. Sometimes Mung, who was about Sandee's age, taught the girls how to say things in her language. But they also played games like 'hide and seek', tag, and 'church'.

Sometimes Gleck played too, and when they played games similar to baseball, where more children were needed, others in the village joined in. All of the children, including Sandee and Kim, had work to do as well. They had to help weed gardens, feed chickens, and even baby-sit, if there were younger ones in the family.

Since Sandee and Kim were in and out of everyone's house, they often had questions to ask at bedtime about what they had seen and heard.

"Why does everyone have that red stuff to chew and to spit, making their teeth and mouth all red?" Kim asked one day. "Even Mung was chewing some of it today. She wanted to give us some to taste, but we just shook our heads and said 'no thank-you'."

"It's called betel-nut," Mom said. "It is a kind of drug or medicine that makes them feel sleepy, or takes away pain, if they have toothache. It does make their teeth look very bad after a while, turning them black. I'm trying to teach them that it's not good to chew it all the time, especially for the young children. Mostly, it is the older people who chew it."

"Some of them smoke pipes too," Kim added. "But they don't like us to see them do it."

"How do you know?" Mom asked.

"Well, they tell us to go away, and they frighten us and we run home."

Mom looked thoughtful for a moment. "It's best not to go back to the place where you were chased away. You did right to come running home. And, Kim, don't go visiting by yourself—only with Sandee or Mung and Dee."

"Not even Granny Smiles? She likes to see us. She tries to tell us stories when she's weaving cloth, and laughs when she sees us play games. Today she showed me how to weave. She is making a dress for me. Sometimes she wants us to sing for her, and we sing 'Jesus Loves Me' and 'Away in a Manger', since it is almost Christmas." Kim looked sad for a moment. "I wish we could have Christmas with Grandma and Grandpa in Canada. I would like to have snow and go sliding and make a snowman."

"I know," Mom said. "That would be lovely. We won't have snow, but we will have a tree. Dad will get a small pine for us to decorate. Would you like to make decorations for it? Maybe Sandee and Mung and Dee would like to do that too. We could make stars and snowflakes from silver and white paper, and red and green paper chains."

But before they could get started, Dad came into the room carrying a huge watermelon. "Look at what Headman Tiger gave me! Anyone want a piece?"

They all sat down to eat the delicious fruit. It was very sweet and juicy, dripping all over their chins and down the front of the girls' t-shirts. Because it was a hot day, it tasted especially good.

"Why don't we all go down to the creek and cool off," Dad suggested. "There's a nice little waterfall up the creek a bit, where we could actually shower. Want to come too, Susan?"

"Yes, let's all go. I'll put the rest of the watermelon in the fridge for later. We'll have biscuits and watermelon for supper."

It was hot and sticky-feeling in the woods. There was a wonderful fragrance coming from the plants and flowers around them. Dad carried a stick, as he usually did, in case they met a snake. Mom carried a towel and soap.

"This is where we saw the elephants," Sandee pointed out to Mom and Dad when they came to the creek, but there was no sign or sound of them now.

"We'll go up the creek a bit farther," Dad told them, "to where the falls are. Listen. Can you hear them?"

Kim and Sandee ran ahead. Mom couldn't walk too fast these days, because soon the baby would be arriving. Dad stayed with her.

The waterfall had made a little pool about a meter deep and three meters across. The water was quite warm and clear. Dad and the girls were wearing shorts and t-shirts and Mom was wearing a loose, cotton dress. They all went into the water with their clothes on, standing under the falls for a shower and shampoo, soaping themselves and their clothes, all over. Then the girls played in the pool, swimming and diving, which they had both learned to do in a pool in Chiang Mai. Dad stayed with them while Mom sat down at the edge of the creek. They were surprised and pleased to see how well Sandee and Kim swam.

Some brightly coloured, noisy birds settled in the trees nearby to watch and, once, Sandee was sure she heard barking deer in the bushes.

"Time to go back," Mom called. "Come out now and I'll towel off your hair and brush it. The rest of you, and your clothes will likely be dry by the time we get to the house. What a lovely way to cool off and do the laundry!"

As they were walking back they met Gleck hurrying along the path leading up from a different part of the creek. He was surprised to see them, but slowed down to walk with them, talking to Dad. When Malcolm asked what he had been doing alone in the forest he didn't answer at first, then said something about hunting. He was carrying a slingshot which could be used to kill birds or small animals, but he didn't have anything in his bag.

"I don't think he was swimming," Sandee commented after Gleck left them. He was wet, but he didn't look clean. I guess he just walked through the water."

"Where the elephants were," Kim added.

"What observant girls you are," Dad said, laughing. "Did you learn that at school too?"

That evening as Sandee and Kim lay in their net-covered beds, listening to the CD Mom and Dad were playing, they talked about all the adventures they had already experienced in the ten days since they came to Tall Pine Village.

"Today was the best," Kim said enthusiastically. "Swimming and showering was such fun! We should do it every day."

"I liked the elephants," Sandee said. "I wish we could see them again. I wonder where they stay and what kind of work they do. Somebody must own them, unless they were wild elephants. I wish we could speak the Karen language so we could find out more."

Just as Sandee was falling asleep Kim whispered, "Where did you put the Christmas presents we brought for Mom and Dad? I was looking for them today and couldn't find them."

"Sh-h. We don't want them to hear. I'll show you in the morning. Now go to sleep." Sandee pulled her blanket around her ears, and Kim snuggled down too, with her Teddy bear.

Chapter Four

Too Many Secrets

AT BREAKFAST the next morning Mom and Dad made plans for the coming week. It was already the eighteenth of December; only six more days till the people from the Striped Creek church would be coming to celebrate Christmas with the Tall Pine village people, who had never celebrated Christmas.

"But where will they sleep and eat?" the girls wondered. "Do we have room for all of them? We don't have a church here."

"It isn't the whole church coming, probably only about four families. I have talked with the villagers and most of them are willing to have some people sleep at their homes," Dad explained. "Some will sleep here, in our front room. They will bring sleeping mats and blankets with them. The celebration itself will be here at our house, but we will put up a kind of tent, so there will be enough room. Everyone will help with the food. It will be like a two-day picnic."

"Are you home?" they heard Mung calling loudly outside.

Sandee and Kim rushed to open the door. Mung and Dee were standing there, holding water buckets. "We're going for water; do you want to come along?" they asked.

"Mom, can we go?" Sandee asked. "We could get some water for you."

"I don't see why not, as long as you all go together," Mom agreed. "We can always use more water."

She gave them each a pail, and the four girls hurried down the path to the well. By now they were able to understand each other pretty well, without actually saying a great deal. Mom stood in the doorway watching the four girls, thinking what a pretty picture they made as they ran off into the brilliantly-green forest.

Kim and Dee, who were about the same size, started running ahead, racing, to see who would get to the well first. Sandee and Mung ran too, to catch up to them. They all arrived at the well at the same time, nearly falling over each other, laughing.

Suddenly Kim pointed at the path and said, "Look, there's Amber. She followed us here. I'd better catch her so she doesn't run off again and get lost."

"Just leave her," Sandee said. "She didn't get lost last time." But Kim was already running down the path towards Amber who, seeming to think this was a game, dashed on down the path towards the creek. The other three watched the chase, then started filling their buckets.

When Kim did not return immediately, Sandee decided to go look for her, leaving her pails on the path. She had only gone a short distance down the path to the creek when Kim came running back, very excited.

"Hurry! Come quick!" she shouted. "The elephants are back and there's a white baby elephant with them. Hurry!"

Without stopping to remember what their parents had said, Sandee ran after Kim. Mung and Dee stared after them, then set down their buckets and ran too. As they neared the creek they could hear a lot of splashing noises, but when they actually got there the elephants were gone.

The girls looked at each other; then all of them began to talk at once, in their own language.

"It must have been elephants," Sandee said. "It certainly sounded like it, but where are they?"

"They've gone, but I saw them," Kim said firmly. "And, see, there are big tracks over there which only elephants could make."

Sandee went over to look. Mung and Dee looked too. Then Mung pointed at some smaller foot-prints beside the big ones. She and Dee started jumping up and down, motioning with their hands, trying to explain to Sandee and Kim.

"I know!" Kim said. "I told you there was a baby elephant. I saw it. It was kind of a whitish-pink colour, not grey like the big ones."

Mung and Dee could not understand everything Kim was saying, but Sandee still didn't believe her.

"Maybe all baby elephants are that colour and turn grey later," Kim said. "Shall we run after them so you can see it?"

"No, we'd better go home now. We're not even supposed to be here," Sandee remembered. "And where's Amber; I hope they didn't step on her."

When they returned to the buckets of water, there was Amber, sitting quietly, licking her paws and washing her face. She followed the girls back to the house.

Sandee and Kim said goodbye to Mung and Dee, then hurried into the house, only spilling a little water.

"Are baby elephants white?" Kim asked, all out of breath.

"Sh-h-h," Sandee said. "Don't."

"What? Baby elephants? What are you talking about?" Mom wanted to know. She looked closely at the two girls, who were suddenly very quiet. "Did you go down to the creek, after we said you should not go there without our permission?"

"Well," Kim began, but Sandee interrupted. "It was Amber's fault. She followed us to the well and when Kim tried to catch her, she ran down the path to the creek and Kim chased her and saw elephants there. The rest of us heard them, but we didn't see any at all, but there must have been a baby one because of the tracks."

"Now listen, you two. This is more serious than you seem to think it is," Mom said sternly. "We told you not to go into the forest by yourselves and you disobeyed. Do you think that was a good thing to do?"

"I'm sorry, Mommy," Kim said. "I forgot, but I should have remembered. But Sandee came to find me—she wasn't disobedient."

"Still, it was wrong. And, blaming Amber is not a good enough excuse, either. What will we do so you will remember next time?" Mom asked. "We don't want you to get lost or hurt. You will have to stay in the house today—no running around the village or anywhere. You can help get the place ready for tomorrow's worship service and make Christmas decorations."

Mom gave Sandee a bucket of soapy water and a brush, with which to scrub the whole outside verandah thoroughly. Kim was given a dusting cloth to clean off the window-sills, benches, chairs and anything else that needed dusting in the bedrooms. After all that was done, and it took quite a while, they got out the paper, scissors and paste to make tree decorations.

"While you were cleaning, during my rest time," Mom told the girls, "I was reading a book called *Stronger than the Strong*, written by one of the first missionaries to come to the Pwo Karen. Her name is Louise Morris. She and her husband Jim were here a long time ago, pioneers, going to Karen villages to learn the language and to tell the people about Jesus."

"Here in this village?", Kim asked.

"No, not this one, because it wasn't here then, but in places like Wangloong, Ming Out Village, Striped Creek, and others, some that no longer exist, since the Pwo Karen moved about quite a bit."

Sandee and Kim giggled. "Why do they have such funny names?"

"Our names sound just as funny to them," Mom pointed out.

Then Sandee added, "In school one day we were told all the names of the hill tribes in Thailand and we tried to memorize them. Let's see if I can still say them. Karen,

Khamu, Lua, Lisu, Lahu, Mien, Mong (Blue and White), Padaung."

"You forgot Akha," Kim said.

"I don't think we learned Akha."

"Yes, you did," said Kim. "That's the first one in the list and the only one I remembered, and you didn't say it."

"And they each speak their own language, you know," Mom continued. "Besides that, there are several kinds of Karen and they also speak different languages. And some of the languages still aren't in writing. Teachers from several countries have been teaching the tribal people to read and write, but then they also have to translate the Bible and other books into that language, so that they will have something to read. It's a lot of hard work and takes a long time."

"Like making your own Christmas decorations," Sandee said. "I think Granny Smiles can read. I saw her looking at a book once when we were there."

"Really?" Mom was surprised. "I wonder where she would have learned. She came to Tall Pine Village from across the mountains, so she couldn't have learned here. When the Striped Creek people come for the Christmas celebrations they are bringing copies of the New Testament in Pwo Karen, which has just been printed, to give to the people here. And, you know what? One of the people who spent years working on that translation is from Canada! Her name is Nancy Stephens. For a while she lived and worked in Prosperity Fields and, later, in Chiang Mai. Didn't they tell you about her at River House?"

"Here comes Dad," Kim announced. "Let me tell him about the white elephant."

Dad was very surprised."Are you sure of what you

saw, Kim? Baby elephants are grey too, so if you really saw a white one it would be an albino; they are very rare."

"And they belong to the king," Sandee suddenly broke in. "When we were reading about the history of Thailand at school there was a story about white elephants. If anybody finds a white elephant, it has to be captured and brought to the king. That's the rule. It brings good luck, or something," she finished.

"Kim, tell me exactly what happened," Dad told her. "Try to remember everything."

"I was chasing Amber, trying to catch her. And when we got to the creek I heard splashing noises, and there was a big elephant and the baby, having a bath. Then I quickly ran to call the others because I thought they would like to see them too. But, by the time we came back again they had gone away."

"But we heard noises," Sandee added, "And we saw tracks in the mud—big and little ones."

"Were they the same elephants you saw before?"

"Just one big one and the baby," Kim said. "We saw two big ones last time. But it could have been one of those."

"This is all very strange," Dad said. "I know there are men working near here, cutting teak wood, who are using elephants—Headman Tiger told me that—but wild ones and a baby? Wouldn't someone out hunting have seen them, especially if it is a white baby elephant? Do you think I should mention it to Headman Tiger, Susan?"

"Maybe we should wait till after Christmas, Malcolm; we don't really want them to all start thinking about something else right now. Why don't we keep it as our secret," Mom suggested, "at least till after the celebrations are over."

"It's pretty hard to keep something as big as an elephant secret, especially if it stays near where everyone gets water. Besides, it might be dangerous. Animals are very protective of their young; we wouldn't want Mung or Dee, or any of the other children hurt."

"Anyway, Mung and Dee saw the tracks too," Sandee said. "They will tell their parents, so it won't be secret."

Dad looked at her. "That's right. And if it was a wild elephant it is probably gone out of this area anyway, because elephants have to keep moving to get their food. Okay, let's leave it for now and get on with other things."

"Too many secrets," Kim said to Sandee as they sat in their beds, ready for bed. "Did you remember to ask God to forgive you for disobeying Mom and Dad?"

"I did," Sandee said, then added, "are you sure the baby elephant was white? Maybe you didn't see it very well."

"I saw very well," Kim said loudly. "I didn't even know there were such things as white elephants, so I must have seen it. I did not make it up. Does it really belong to the king of Thailand? Then shouldn't we let him know it's here? Did it escape?"

"I don't think he would have had this one yet, so he wouldn't know about it. But if he finds out about it, then he will want it," Sandee tried to explain.

"We could write him a letter," Kim said, hesitantly.

"But maybe he wouldn't believe us, since only you saw it and you're only eight."

"Maybe we could get a picture," Kim said, "if we saw it again."

"Go to sleep now, girls," Mom called. "We can hear you talking. I'll put on some music."

They both lay down and pulled their blankets around themselves. A moment later Kim whispered, "You didn't tell me where you put the presents for Mom and Dad, Sandee."

"They're in this room. I hid them up on the board under the roof above my bed. Everywhere else Mom would have seen them. I'll show you in the morning."

Chapter Five

Christmas
Excitement

THE NEXT couple of days were very busy ones, as the whole Green family got ready for Christmas celebrations. Dad, with some help from two of the village men, built a wooden platform near their house, which would be the floor for the tent-church where the celebrations would be centered. There was a good deal of hammering and cheerful talk, with children running around and getting in the way.

Mom called some of the children into the house to help make decorations for the tent-church. There were brightly coloured balloons to blow up, paper chains to get ready, and stars to cut out of gold and silver paper. There was a small pine tree too, which was a special treat for Kim and Sandee. They decorated the tree with red bells and silver

stars and, underneath the tree, was a tiny manger scene, with Mary and Joseph and the baby Jesus.

All the village people were getting ready for visitors; even the ones who said they would not invite anyone to stay at their house, were coming to see the platform being built, and listening to the talk. Most of the food was being brought by the visitors, but Susan had also baked cookies and cake to share, which would be a new treat for the Pwo Karen people. There would be spicy chicken stew and other delicious foods with hot peppers, and lots of sticky rice. Granny Smiles brought a basket of freshly roasted peanuts as a snack for the workers and children.

At Susan's invitation she sat down on their porch to drink tea and to watch the children making decorations. She peered at the little tree and the creche beneath it, but didn't say anything.

"Where did you get the peanuts, Granny?" Kim asked. "They're the best I've ever tasted."

"Why, from my garden, of course," Granny told her, getting up after finishing her tea. "Why don't you children come along to help me get some cabbages and I'll show you how my peanuts grow."

"Can we go, Mommy?" Sandee and Kim asked.

"Yes you may go, if you promise to come right back here afterwards; no running off into the forest. And don't stay too long, because there are still things to be done here."

Mung and Dee decided to go along too. They all helped carry Granny's baskets. The big gardens where the villagers grew their cabbages, carrots, peppers and peanuts were in one large field, a short distance from the rice fields, though most of the families grew some vegetables and fruits near their houses too.

Some other people were also gathering vegetables from their gardens, or pulling weeds. Granny cut two large cabbages to take home, as well as some carrots and a pumpkin. She showed Sandee and Kim the peanut plants, which were about a foot high, and pulled one up to show them the peanuts growing under the earth. Kim wanted to taste them, but Mung laughed and said you couldn't eat them till they were roasted or cooked. The girls helped to harvest a small basketful of peanuts.

As they were leaving the field, Mung pointed excitedly towards the edge of the field. A deer was feeding there! The children started to run towards it, but the deer heard them and quickly vanished into the forest. Immediately, Sandee and Kim stopped and headed back to Granny Smiles, remembering their promise. As they started back, they were surprised to see Gleck get up from the ground not far from where they had seen the deer. He did not seem happy to see them, and told them to go away. His sisters asked him what he was doing there, but he wouldn't answer. Sandee noticed he had his slingshot and a big stick. Then, Granny called them to come, and they went to help her carry the vegetables home. She watched them as they ran towards her.

"Was that Gleck over there?" Granny asked Mung, who nodded. "Why is he not with the other boys? I must speak to his mother about this." She kept grumbling about Gleck as they walked along, paying no attention to the happy chatter of the four girls.

After they had helped carry the baskets of vegetables

to Granny Smiles' house, Sandee and Kim said good-bye and hurried home.

"Why was Granny angry at Gleck?" Kim wondered, as they walked along. "And why did he chase us away from the flower field?"

"Flowers? I didn't see any flowers. I thought he was watching the deer. Maybe he was hunting again. He did kill a snake one day. Mung said they ate it for their supper. Yuch! I wouldn't eat a snake!"

"You would if it was in a stew," Kim told her. "Remember? We had frog stew and it was good. Oh look, the platform is all finished!"

The men had left and Dad was helping Mom with the cleaning up that needed to be done in the living room. Mom looked very tired. Kim immediately began to tell them about the peanuts, and the deer, and Gleck.

"Did you say Gleck was near a flower field?" Dad interrupted her. "What kind of flowers?"

"I didn't see any flowers," Sandee said. "Kim is always seeing things no one else sees."

"I do not! There were flowers, lots of them—all the same kind. I think they are called poppies. Gleck was sitting there and he told us to go away."

"Was it the same field where the man chased us away when we were watching people harvesting rice?" Dad asked.

"I think so; probably, but only Gleck was there this time," Sandee said.

"It sounds as if someone is growing poppies for opium," Dad said. "That's probably why they don't want us to go near there; they know it's against the law. But

Gleck is only a young boy; why would he be involved? Susan, I think we should pray for him right now, that he will be protected against harm and danger."

They all four sat down, held hands, and prayed for Gleck, and also for whoever was planting the poppies.

"We should try to get to bed early tonight," Mom suggested, when they had finished praying. "Tomorrow by lunch-time the visitors will be arriving; from then on till they leave, the day after Christmas, we'll be going non-stop."

"Good idea, Susan, you sit still, while the girls and I finish up."

There wasn't much left to be done, only the chickens to be fed and given water and their nests checked for eggs, and vegetables to be brought in from their garden for their supper.

After supper, Dad looked at the platform again, to make sure it was finished and in good order. He had just come in, as it was getting dark, when they heard a loud noise outside, like fire-crackers going off. Then something was thrown against their door! The cats, who were sleeping, jumped up and tried to hide; even the chickens, shut in their shed for the night, squawked loudly.

Malcolm switched on the powerful flashlight he kept for emergencies and called, "Who's there?"

No one answered. When he opened the door after a few minutes of listening, he found a large stone on the porch, but whoever had thrown it was gone. He looked and listened to see if anyone was hiding nearby, but could not see anyone. Nothing had been damaged, so he shut the door again, bolting it on the inside.

Sandee and Kim were getting ready for bed. Dad made

sure their shutters were firmly closed and their mosquito nets tucked in.

"I'll play some Christmas music for you," he said. "Think about Christmas in Canada, and remember God is protecting us here just as he did when we were there."

"But people didn't throw rocks at us there," Sandee reminded him.

"People do bad things there too," Dad said. "We all need God to change our hearts. Go to sleep now; I'll stay up and read for a while."

There were no other loud noises, only the shrill, rasping noise of cicadas and other night sounds.

The next thing Kim and Sandee noticed was light shining into their window, and Mom saying breakfast was nearly ready. While they were getting dressed and making their beds, Sandee reached up to the hiding place above her bed and pulled out the presents for their parents.

"Here they are, see, Kim?" she whispered. "Today is Christmas Eve; shall we give them their presents today, or wait till the visitors are gone?"

"Let's wait, but we can tell them we have presents for them so they won't be disappointed. Do you think they have presents for us?"

Sandee pushed the presents back into their hiding place. "I suppose so, but maybe they didn't have time to get us anything. Maybe the cats were our present."

By the time breakfast was over children from the village were already playing games on the new platform beside their house and on the Green's porch, looking in at the window to see if Sandee and Kim were finished eating. Some of the grown-ups came over too, to help set up an outside cooking-fire, on which they placed a huge iron pot, to cook stew for the noon meal. Most of the preparations for this meal were done in the Green's front room, but several of the village women were helping. Other families were cooking sticky rice to bring for the meal.

Granny Smiles came to see how the preparations were going, and to make sure that the right ingredients were being put in. She called Kim over, reached into her basket and pulled out a beautiful white dress with pink and red trimmings. She held it up against Kim to see if it fit. Then she pulled out another dress exactly like the first one, but bigger, for Sandee.

"Granny Smiles, did you make these for my girls?" Mom asked. "They are beautiful!"

"I told you Granny was making a dress for me." Kim laughed as she hugged the dress to herself. She gave Granny a big hug too.

"You can wear them for the celebrations," Granny said, "then you will be Karen girls."

"Go hang them up in your room now," Mom told the girls. "You can wear them when the celebrations begin. Now run along and play outside, children. We can't get any work done with so many in here."

"Let's play hide-and-seek," Mung suggested. "Or tag—I'll race you to Headman Tiger's house."

She took off at full speed, with the rest of the children trying to catch up, but she was much faster than all of them. Mrs. Tiger was getting rice ready to cook. She did not want twenty children in her house.

"Here, you, Mung!" she called. "Do something useful. I need more water to cook this rice. Why don't you children fetch water for me. Come here." She gave them two pails and an empty pot to carry. All the children decided to go along to the well, while the bigger ones carried the pails.

"Don't drop them now, or spill the water on your-selves," Mrs. Tiger called after them.

Still laughing and running, they all followed the path to the well, tripping over each other as the bigger girls tried to fill the pails. Mung and Sandee, who were the biggest, were getting angry.

"Stop being so silly," Sandee said, stamping her foot. "You sound like a bunch of monkeys."

"More like a lot of elephants," Mung added. Then, remembering the elephant tracks they had seen, she added, "No, even elephants wouldn't be this loud. We didn't even hear them at the creek till we were right there, remember?"

"Let's go see the elephants," Dee said. "Let's go see if they are there again."

"No, we can't," Kim said quickly. "We promised we wouldn't go there alone again, Sandee."

"But we didn't promise," Mung and Dee said.

"Well, we're not going," Sandee said, picking up one of the pails. "Besides, Mrs. Tiger needs this water." She and Kim started back to the village. The other children hesitated for a moment, then they picked up the rest of the water containers and followed, more quietly this time.

Mrs. Tiger thanked them for the water and told them to find something else to do.

Sandee and Kim started back to their house, while the rest of the children continued into the village. Amber and Jasper were stalking a bird near their house. The girls stopped to watch what would happen. A long snake slithered across the path a short distance in front of them. The cats saw it coming and jumped out of the way, hissing. It disappeared into the grass. Kim shivered, then called the cats, but they went back to their hunt.

"I'm going in," Kim decided, "to wait till the visitors come. I hope they come soon cause I'm getting awfully hungry. That stew in the pot sure smells yummy."

It was not long before a shout of, "Here they come!" was heard, followed by the sound of a motor, as first one truck arrived, and then a Land-Rover and another truck, all full of people, came into view.

Malcolm and Susan, Headman Tiger and his wife, who came hurrying, and others still there, greeted the visitors and helped them to unload. The Striped Creek people had brought a tent to put over the bamboo poles around the platform, as well as sound equipment, which had to be set up. They brought food to share too, and a couple of parcels and other mail for the Greens.

Sandee and Kim were thrilled to see the parcels from their grandparents. Dad put the parcels and all the other mail in his bedroom, and told the girls they would have to wait till next morning to open them. Even then there probably would not be much time to do it, because of everything else happening.

"We'll have a family Christmas after everybody leaves, I promise," he told them, noticing their disappointment.

Soon a parade of villagers came to the Green house, carrying trays of sticky rice to share with the guests. Everyone sat down on mats on the floor, inside the tent and on the Green's verandah and front room, around the large trays. Each tray had a bowl of stew in the centre and piles of sticky rice around it for each person. As, together, they ate the rice, shaped into balls and dipped into the hot stew, they got to know each other.

Most of the Striped Creek people were strangers to the Tall Pine villagers, but all of them were from the Pwo Karen tribes.

When everyone had finished eating and the trays were cleaned up, it was time to start the celebration. The sound system was turned on, playing music as a signal for the people to gather in the tent. For this evening meeting everyone would be together; on Christmas day some special activities were planned for the children. Mothers with babies brought them along; the children, including Sandee and Kim in their new dresses, crowded near the front of the platform. Almost all the villagers came to see what these Christians from Striped Creek would do and say.

A small choir began the program by singing Christmas songs and then teaching them to the villagers. They brought out song books, with the words in the Karen language, for those who could read. It did not take long till everyone was at least trying to sing. Since Sandee and Kim knew the songs in English, they sang them that way.

After the singing, there were skits performed by the visitors explaining why there is Christmas, and how the coming of the baby Jesus changed everything. There were more songs and then, when it was dark, they showed a movie about the life of Jesus. After that, the children were all taken home to sleep, the visitors also going to the homes to which they had been invited, carrying their sleeping mats. But some of the men stayed to talk in the tent. Sandee and Kim could hear their voices till they fell asleep.

Chapter Six

Presents and Surprises

SANDEE WAS the first to awake. Their rooster was crowing loudly already, but it was still quite dark in their bedroom. She listened for sounds of anyone being up, but there were no such sounds. Kim was still sleeping. Carefully, Sandee reached up to the hiding place and pulled out the presents hidden there. She and Kim had bought them in the market at Chiang Mai. She opened the cardboard box they were in, and took out the tiny carved animals—an elephant and a tiger—feeling their smooth animal shapes, smelling the carefully shaped wood. They were beautiful! Would Mom and Dad like them too?

"Kim, wake up; it's Christmas!" Sandee whispered. "Wake up! We can open the parcel from Grandpa and Grandma now."

Kim sat up, rubbing her eyes, but she was wide awake in a moment and started crawling out from under the mosquito netting.

"Sh-h, be very quiet. We don't want to wake the people sleeping on the floor."

They tiptoed past the sleeping people, Sandee carrying the carved animals, and went into their parents' room. Since they were sleeping soundly Sandee placed the animals on the table beside their bed, then reached for the big parcel from the grandparents. They sat down at the foot of the bed and began to remove the wrappings. Inside was a box with a number of wrapped presents. They quickly found one which had their names on it.

"Let me, Sandee, let me open it," Kim said, holding out her hands.

"Well, okay, but be careful." Sandee watched as another box appeared, with writing on it; inside was a Polaroid camera and four film packs. "For Sandee and Kim, so they can take pictures to show us when they come to visit," read the note from Grandma and Grandpa. Inside the box was a little book explaining how to take pictures and develop them.

Mom sat up, surprised to see the girls. She shook Dad to wake him too. Sandee held up the camera to show them.

"How does it work, Dad?" Kim asked. Sandee was already reading the directions.

"Here, give it to me," Mom said. "I had one like that when I was a girl. I'll take a picture of the two of you and show you how it works." She focussed the camera, pressed the shutter, and in less than a minute, showed them the finished picture.

"Hey, that's cool!" Sandee said. "We can take pictures of the celebration and the village and..."

"And don't forget, Sandee, Grandpa and Grandma want us to put them in an album to show them when we visit, or if they visit us, and I think this next package, with our name on it, is an album."

"Wait a minute," Dad said. "I said one present to open today. That's it. Now stop! Save the rest for tomorrow!" Then he noticed the tiger and elephant standing on their bedside table. "What's this? Where did these wild animals come from?" He picked up the crouching tiger and examined it, then did the same to the elephant, while the girls watched. "These are very well-crafted animals, Susan. How did they get here? Did you find them somewhere?"

Kim couldn't wait any longer. "They're from us! Sandee and I picked them out in the Chiang Mai market. They were the best ones we could find for five baht."

"They are beautiful!" Mom told them. "Really beautiful; thank you!"

"Five baht, hm-m, not bad," Dad said.

"Each!" added Sandee. "We had to bargain. He wanted twenty!"

"I'm impressed," said Dad. "Our girls keep surprising me," said Dad to Mom, his eyes twinkling. "What will they do next?"

"Wait and see," said Sandee, laughing.

"Listen," whispered Mom. "I think I hear our guests waking up. We'd better get dressed quickly and help make breakfast."

Soon one of the men bonged the gong outside their house, to call people to come for breakfast. Again, families brought their trays, and food was distributed to everyone. One of the Christians from Striped Creek thanked God for the food and the new day.

After they all had enough to eat, they met for more singing, and then there was a surprise! A large cardboard box was brought into the tent and, while everyone watched, Malcolm explained that inside the box was a wonderful gift for them. He opened the box and pulled out a book—a New Testament, written in the Pwo Karen language! He explained that many years had been spent translating this book into their language. Many people, both Karen and missionaries, had spent hours and hours working on it, and now it was finally finished. Then, one person from each family was given a copy to keep. All the people were very excited, even though some of them still couldn't read.

Then the children were taken to the verandah of the Green house for stories and crafts, while the rest of the people met for teaching from the New Testament and were shown how to read it.

Sandee and Kim listened to the stories for the children too, but since it was all in Pwo Karen, they could not understand everything. They had taken a picture of Dad handing out the New Testaments, and of the children on their porch, with the decorations they had made and the little tree they had trimmed, in the background.

Suddenly Kim had an idea. "Let me have the camera, Sandee," she whispered.

"What for?" Sandee whispered back.

Kim hesitated a moment, then she whispered, "Come with me and I'll show you. Sh-h. We don't want anyone to see us go."

Since the teacher was telling an exciting story just then, not even Mung noticed Sandee and Kim leave. Kim led the way, running quickly along the path to the gardens. When they were out of sight of their house, she slowed down. "I want to take a picture of the poppies to show Dad," Kim told Sandee. "Then he'll believe that I really saw them."

"But what if Gleck is there again? I didn't see him at the celebration today," Sandee said.

"We'll have to go very quietly and bend down so he won't see us, if he's there," Kim said. "And take the picture quickly. Maybe we should go through the gardens instead of along the path."

"Yes, that's a good idea," Sandee agreed, "but we mustn't step on the plants, so be careful."

Crouching and walking carefully, they soon came within sight of the poppies—a whole patch of them. Kim focussed the camera carefully and took a picture which Sandee helped her develop. It was a good picture, clearly showing the poppies. Then they saw Gleck. He was getting up from the ground where he must have been sitting, and he looked straight at them. Quickly, he came toward them, waving his arms and shouting! Kim started to run and Sandee followed her. They ran towards the edge of the field where the woods were, trying to hide from Gleck who was still following. They burst into the forest without even thinking of the dangers that might be there. A stone flew past them, and they kept running.

Suddenly, right there in front of them was the white baby elephant! Both girls stopped in astonishment, but Kim, who was still carrying the camera, immediately snapped a picture and handed it to Sandee to develop. The little elephant had not seemed to notice them, but now it waved its trunk around and then faced right towards them. Kim took another picture. Then they heard loud elephant-trumpeting coming from the river, a short distance farther into the forest, and were startled to hear the little elephant make a very loud noise too. It started running toward its mother.

Terrified, Kim and Sandee grabbed each other. Then they turned to see if Gleck was still chasing them, but they could not see anyone. "Shall we follow the baby elephant?" Kim whispered. "Wasn't it loud!"

"I think we'd better go home. The mother elephant might try to hurt us if she thinks we're bothering her baby. I don't want her roaring at us. Let's try to go through the woods, so Gleck won't see us again."

Still afraid that Gleck might come to look for them, especially if he had noticed the camera, they tried to walk quietly, and carefully, so as not to get lost.

"Are you sure this is the right direction?" Kim asked after they had pushed through bushes for a while.

Sandee stopped. "Listen. Isn't that the waterfall where we bathed? Let's go towards that sound. We can follow the path back from there," she said, already leading the way.

"Have you got the pictures safe, Sandee?" Kim asked again.

"Yes, they're right here in my hand. I don't have a pocket."

They stopped every few steps to listen for the waterfall and, in a short while, they could see the light shining on the water. Finding the path was easy then. They hurried along the path, past the well, and on towards their house, where the morning sessions were completed and the noon meal was about to begin. Almost at once Sandee and Kim were surrounded by people, exclaiming at their return and their dusty appearance.

"Your parents were looking for you," Mung told them. "Where did you go?"

But the girls didn't want to talk to anyone except their parents, so they hurried into the house and went straight into the parents' bedroom, where they found Mom. She jumped up and gave a little scream when she saw them. They could see she had been crying.

"Where were you? We were so worried; we thought you had been kidnapped. Your Dad and some of the men are looking for you."

Sandee started to explain, but Susan just hugged them and said how glad she was that they were safe. "We'd better let everyone know, so we can get back to the celebrations," she said, wiping her eyes. "Put the camera away. What were you doing? No, I don't have time to look at pictures now. Go change your clothes; your nice new dresses are all dirty. Then come and eat; we'll hear all about it later."

A moment later, the gong rang out to let everyone know that Sandee and Kim were safe. "We'd better hide the camera and the pictures till we can show them to Dad," Sandee said. "We must not lose them. Let's take them to our room. Mom said to change our clothes; hurry Kim."

They managed to slip into their room without attracting attention, hid the pictures and camera under Sandee's mattress, and quickly changed clothes. Then, they went outside to find a place to eat. Granny Smiles, sitting on a mat on the porch, invited them to sit by her tray. They ate greedily; running through the woods had made them very hungry and thirsty.

Malcolm returned and hurried onto the porch to see the girls. He looked hot, but relieved. Since everyone was more or less finished eating, it was time for a short rest before the afternoon and evening sessions would begin. There would be more singing, teaching, skits, and another movie later.

When most of the people had gone to their homes, and their guests were resting, Dad came into the girls' bedroom to find out what had happened. Quickly Sandee got out the camera and the pictures they had hidden, and handed them to him. Puzzled, Dad looked at the pictures one by one. Then, suddenly realizing what he was seeing, he whistled softly, and said, "You were right on both counts, Kim. That is really an albino elephant, and there is Gleck sitting right by the poppy field! Where did you— how did you know where the elephants were? Where exactly is this?"

As Sandee and Kim explained, Dad listened very thoughtfully. Then he handed the pictures back to Sandee and told her to hide them well, and also to hide the camera in a different place.

"We can't do anything till tomorrow, but meanwhile I want you two to stay right at home—don't go to anyone's place, or anywhere else, and stay together, close to Mom or Granny Smiles. It's just possible that Gleck will report you to someone else and there might be trouble. Now, try to have a quiet rest here till you hear the gong."

Kim and Sandee didn't think they would be able to rest, but they actually fell asleep almost right away. They didn't wake up till Mom came into their room to make sure they were there. The gong had already sounded and the people were gathering for the last part of the Christmas celebrations.

"I want you to sit with me," their mother told them. "We'll stay on our verandah from which we can hear and see well."

A Christmas-music tape was playing as the people gathered again to hear what the Striped Creek people would teach. This time there was mostly singing, with some of the young people playing the guitar to accompany the songs, but everyone was invited to sing along. Kim joined in the singing, but Sandee was watching the people. As it was getting dark she saw Gleck coming along the path to their house. She slid a little closer to Mom, but watched to see where he would go. He looked toward them as he walked by, but went on to where some other boys were sitting.

Then, it was time for the movie. Granny Smiles came onto the porch to sit near them, so did Amber and Jasper. Sandee took Jasper on her lap and soon he was purring happily. Sandee looked up at the sky where stars were beginning to glow. She remembered that in Canada she had always looked for the Big Dipper when she was outside at night, but here she looked for the Southern Cross, and now she could see it shining brightly.

The movie had ended. Mothers and children were getting up to go to their sleeping places. Some people were staying to talk. Mom got up and went in to put the kettle on for tea for the people sleeping at the Green house. Sandee shook Jasper off her lap as she got up to go in. Kim was so sleepy that Sandee had to shake her too. She looked up quickly at the sound of a loud hiss directly below her. Jasper jumped and hissed too. A boy's voice whispered harshly, "Don't come near me again or you'll be in big trouble."

Granny Smiles, who was slowly pulling herself up, heard the voice too. She peered into the darkness. "Gleck, is that you? What has come over that boy," she muttered, as she received no answer.

"Hurry Kim," Sandee said, "let's go to bed quickly. It's not safe out here."

"Don't worry, child," Granny said. "Didn't we just hear that God loves and cares for us? He is stronger than the evil one. Yes, that is so," she repeated aloud, as she walked home with the other people.

Chapter Seven

The Missing Camera

THE WHOLE village was up at daybreak the next morning. The tent had to be taken down, breakfast made and eaten quickly, and all the equipment, mats, and pots loaded onto the trucks, as the Striped Creek people got ready to leave. Malcolm loaded some things into the Land-Rover, as he prepared to go back with them, taking three people in his car.

"I'll be back well before dark," he told Susan and the girls. "I will have to drive to Hod to the government representative there to show him your pictures, but I'll come right back. Sandee and Kim, be sure to stay with your mother all day; she needs more rest."

They waved from the porch as the trucks and Rovers left, then went inside to eat their own breakfast.

"You know what," Mom said, noticing that the girls were both looking very glum, "why don't we open the rest of the presents your grandparents sent. We haven't really had time to do any family things with all the people here."

Kim and Sandee brightened up at once, especially after Mom assured them that Dad wouldn't mind.

"We'll put the little tree here on the table so we can see it and think about how your grandparents will be spending Christmas," Mom said, placing the tree and straightening the decorations. "Sandee, get the parcels from our bedroom while I put on a Christmas CD."

Kim and Sandee took turns opening the wrapped presents. There were books, two games—Jenga and chess, hard wrapped candy, some new clothes, an album for the pictures they would take, and even cake mixes for them to bake, as well as presents for Mom and Dad.

"Mom, can we bake the chocolate cake for supper today?" Sandee wondered. "We haven't had chocolate for a long time."

"I think so," Susan said. "We'll need a couple of eggs though. Our hens have been kept so busy providing eggs for our visitors that I wonder if there are any left. In fact, we really should check to see if they have water to drink."

"We'll go," Kim said. "Come on, Sandee." She picked up the egg basket and headed out the door. Sandee brought a gourd of water from the large pots outside, where they kept water for hens and for cleaning or laundry. Dad had filled them before he left. They found five newly-laid eggs.

As they climbed the steps up to their porch they heard a shout, and Mung and Dee came running.

"Come play with us," Mung invited them. "We're going to the river with our mother to help wash laundry and to play in the water."

"No, we can't," Sandee said quickly. "We have to help our mother in the house today."

"We have new games," Kim added, "When you come back you could come play here with us."

As they ran down the path to the river, Kim watched wistfully.

"Never mind," Sandee said. "We'll go again with Dad. We promised to stay with Mom, remember. We can help bake the cake and make a Christmas supper for Dad."

"Why is Dad going to Hod with my pictures? I thought the King lived in Bangkok?" Kim asked.

"Well he does," Sandee agreed, "but he has people working for him in Hod and they can telephone the king and see if he wants the elephant captured and brought to him."

When they came into the living-room Mom was sitting there reading Christmas letters, which they also had not had time to read before. They were barely in the house when they heard someone calling, "Are you home?"

Mom got up slowly and looked out. One of the village women was there. "Can you come right away," she asked, anxiously. "My neighbor's baby is very sick—can't eat. The Headman came to see what he could do, but it hasn't helped."

"Yes, of course I'll come," Susan said. She went to get her medicine kit, then noticing Sandee and Kim watching, said, "You'll have to come with me. I need your help."

Susan asked a few more questions of the woman to

find out exactly what was wrong with the baby, but she only said: "You will see," and then walked quickly along.

The house they came to was on the edge of the village: quite a small, poorly built house. They all went up onto the porch, but Sandee and Kim waited outside while Mom and the other woman went in. There were a few hens scratching around in a small pen near the house, but no pigs or other animals. The porch was not very clean, so the girls didn't feel like sitting down. It seemed a long time till Mom finally came out. The other woman stayed inside.

"What's that thing by the door, Mom?" Kim asked, pointing at something made of bent twigs.

Mom looked surprised when she saw what Kim was pointing at. "Oh dear," she said. "We'd better go home quickly now." And she did not say anything more till they were some distance away from the house. Then she said, "That was a sign which meant no one was supposed to go into the house, put there by either Headman Tiger or, maybe, the father of the baby. I didn't see it when I went in. But the woman who called me must have known." After a moment she added: "The baby is very sick, but we prayed together and I gave her medicine, and told them how to care for her. Still, the father will be angry if he hears that I was there."

When they came to their own house they noticed at once that something was wrong. The chickens were making angry, squawking noises; Amber and Jasper were hiding under the house and came out with their tails up and very bushy, and their front door was partly open.

"Is anyone there?" Susan called loudly. When they heard nothing, Sandee ran up the steps and pushed the door wide open. Susan and Kim followed more slowly, but they all stared at the mess they saw. Someone had thrown things around, opened cupboard doors, even pulled pillows, mosquito netting and blankets out of place, but there was no one there now.

Susan closed the front door and locked it. "Who could have done this? And why?" she wondered. "Is anything missing? We'd better clean up and see if anything has been stolen."

They put things back into cupboards, checked to see that the Christmas presents were still there, swept up the remains of one cake mix that had been dumped, and re-made the beds.

"The camera!" Kim said. "Where's our camera? Did Dad take it along?"

"No, he took the pictures you developed, but not the camera. Where did you keep it?"

"In our bedroom," Sandee said, running to check. "I had it in the bedside table, but it's not there now."

"Then it must be Gleck," Kim said. "He wants the pictures we took. He must have seen us take the pictures after all."

"But how did he know we were not here? Is he watching our house now, instead of the poppies?" Sandee wondered.

"I think we're in big trouble," Kim said. "I wish Dad were here."

"Well, he's not, but God is," Mom said firmly. "We don't have to be afraid. Let's bake that cake now so it will be ready to eat when Dad comes back. I see the eggs are not broken, at least. Come on, Kim, you can do the mixing."

Chapter Eight

Dad Talks to Headman Tiger

THE CHOCOLATE cake was baked and iced, and supper was nearly ready when they heard the roar of the Land-Rover approaching. Sandee had barely opened the door before Dad was on the porch, bringing an armful of groceries with him.

"Here I am," he announced, smiling. "Why was the door closed? Is that chocolate cake I smell? Am I ever hungry! Wait till I tell you what happened!"

But before he could say anything else, Sandee and Kim told him, both speaking at once, with Mom nodding in agreement, about everything that had happened to them. He listened until they had finished.

"Let's eat supper now, Mother," he said quietly. "While we're eating I'll tell you what I found out. After supper I will go talk to Headman Tiger. He'll want to know what's going on."

"Did you show the pictures to the king?" Kim wanted to know.

"Not to the king, but I did show them to the man in charge of the government office in Hod. He became very excited when he saw the white elephant. At first he couldn't believe it was real, but when he saw the two pictures you took he asked a lot of questions. Then, he told me to wait while he made a phone call to Bangkok. They were very interested and said King Bhumibol Adulyadej would immediately send soldiers out here to see if they can find the elephant and the mother. They might get here tomorrow." Dad got up. "I will talk to Headman Tiger now, so he will know what's happening. Perhaps the village men can help too. Do you need more water, Susan, or can it wait till tomorrow?"

"We have enough," Susan told him. "We'll do the dishes while you're gone, and then get ready for bed."

But, Sandee and Kim were too excited to sleep and were still awake when Dad came back much later.

"What a mess!" They heard Dad say to Mom. "All kinds of secrets are coming out now. I showed Headman Tiger the picture of Gleck at the poppy-field, and told him about our break-in. The man who is growing the poppies is involved in an opium-smuggling ring. Headman Tiger knew about it—probably gets some of the money, though he didn't say that. He had heard something about a white elephant, but had not seen it nor has anyone else in the village. He didn't want to report it, because he was afraid of soldiers coming here and finding out about the opium.

Apparently Gleck was being paid to keep us away from the poppy field—and it was Gleck who searched through our place, trying to find the pictures. He took the camera and still has it. Oh yes, the man who is at the centre of all this is the father of the baby you saw today."

"That explains why he didn't want us to come to his house. What is Headman Tiger going to do? Are we going to be attacked again?" Mom asked. "Is it safe to stay here?"

"I think we're safe. They won't attack when they know the king's men are coming. Headman Tiger didn't say a great deal, but I could tell he was thinking hard. He's probably having a meeting with some of the men right now to decide what to do. Of course, he wasn't pleased that I had gone to Hod, but he knows that I didn't show the soldiers the poppy picture; I only showed them the elephant pictures."

"Will Gleck go to jail?" Sandee asked.

"Are you still awake?" Dad asked. "No, I don't think they put children in jail. I don't know what will happen; we'll have to wait to see what action Headman Tiger will take."

"Dad," Kim said. "You have a secret that you told us not to tell."

"I do?"

"Yes. Remember? Something you bought in Hod. Did you give it to Mom?"

"You're right! I completely forgot! Thanks for reminding me, Kim. Now, where did I put it?" They could hear him searching around. "Here it is. I'm glad Gleck didn't find it. Susan, I'm terribly sorry it's so late, but here is your Christmas present."

"Oh Malcolm, what a lovely necklace! I love the Karen silver-work and this one is beautifully made. I thought you had forgotten all about presents."

"Now it is really time to get to sleep!" Dad told the girls. "I'll turn out the light. We can all pray that God will keep us safe and help us with what happens tomorrow."

Chapter Nine

A Gift for the King

AT DAYBREAK, roosters all over Tall Pine village began to crow. Sandee was already awake. She had been dreaming about elephants—a whole herd of white elephants bathing in the river, with Sandee and Kim watching. Suddenly, they all started trumpeting and the noise woke her up. She sat up in bed and listened. Nothing. Then the roosters started, but she knew there had been something else. Then Kim stirred, and behind the matting-wall Dad was getting dressed and telling Mom to stay in bed and rest.

Sandee got out of the netting cave of her bed and went through to the front room and onto the porch, where Dad was washing his face. Glancing towards the village she could see men going to Headman Tiger's house. Then she

heard another noise, coming from the sky. She and Dad hurried to the front of the porch to get a better look. A helicopter was moving over the hills and forests.

"They are not wasting any time," Dad said. "So that's how they will look for the white elephant; I wondered how they would do it."

The men at Headman Tiger's house had also heard the helicopter. Some of them began to run along the path to the gardens; others seemed to be talking excitedly, but stayed there.

"We'd better have breakfast and get our chores done. I'm sure there will be soldiers coming by truck too, before very long," Dad said. "Go get dressed and get Kim up. We'll need your help."

The helicopter swept over a wide area, circling back and forth, and then hovered directly over the village, before heading back towards Hod.

About an hour later, after the Greens had finished breakfast, they heard a truck approaching. Since their house was the first one on the trail, the truck stopped directly in front of it. Malcolm went out to meet them, while Sandee and Kim watched from the porch. The officer in charge talked to Malcolm in the Thai language, asking questions about exactly where the elephant had been seen, who saw it, and so on.

Malcolm told him what he knew and then suggested he talk to Headman Tiger. Maybe the men in the village could help with finding and catching the elephants, he said. He walked with the men to Headman Tiger's house.

Mung and Dee came running towards the Green house. Sandee and Kim waited to see what they would say. As soon as they got to the steps leading up to the porch, Mung held up Sandee and Kim's camera.

"Gleck told us to give it back to you," Mung said. "Here."

Sandee took it and looked it over to see if it was damaged. It seemed in perfect condition.

"Take a picture, Sandee; then we'll know if it works," Kim suggested.

Sandee took a picture of Mung, Dee and Kim. It developed clearly, just as before.

Dad came back, walking quickly. "Sandee, Kim, you'll have to come along to show the men exactly where you saw the white elephant, since you're the only ones who saw it. Tell Mom you're coming with me."

Kim ran into the bedroom to tell Mom and to give her the camera to keep safe. Then she hurried after Dad and Sandee.

First the girls led the men down to the river. There still were elephant tracks to be seen there, but not very new ones. Then they led the whole troop, and some of the village men down the hill to the gardens, right up to the spot where they had taken the poppy picture. They stopped and looked in that direction.

"Dad, they're gone!" Kim said. "The pop..."

"Sh-h," said Dad. "We'll discuss it later."

The girls turned and led the way into the forest right up to the spot where they had seen the elephant the second time. They noticed that the officer had a photocopy of their picture, at which he looked, when they told him that this was the spot. Sure enough, they found tracks there too, which they followed to the river nearby, but then they disappeared. They all went back to Headman Tiger's house for another meeting, and Sandee and Kim ran home.

"Mom," Kim shouted as soon as they were in the house, "the poppies are all gone! The field was all dug over with nothing there!"

"Well, I'm not surprised," Mom said. "Headman Tiger must have told the men to dig it up, because it's against the law to grow opium, and with the soldiers coming here they knew there would be trouble."

A little while later the truck roared off, and Dad came into the house. "They'll be back tomorrow, and the helicopter will be back too. They're going to bring in an elephant specialist—a person who knows how to capture and train elephants, to take charge. But, they still have to find the elephants, so the men of the village are supposed to see if they can track them down today, and report where they are—probably keep someone there to watch them, but not to spook or harm them," Dad explained.

"Oh, this is so exciting," Kim said, jumping around. "But how can they catch them and take them to Bangkok? The mother is awfully big."

"Don't ask me," said Dad. "That's what the specialist is for. Say, is that your camera?"

"Yes, Dad," Sandee told him, "Mung and Dee brought it. Gleck told them to do it."

"Yes, I thought he would, if he hadn't smashed it. Is it working?"

Sandee showed him the picture she had taken.

Mom came out of the bedroom carrying her medicine bag. "I should go see if the sick baby is getting better," she said. "Kim, I'd like you to come with me, and Sandee, you could help Dad fetch water; our big jugs need filling."

Dad and Sandee had just brought the first load of water when Kim and Mom were back too.

"They're gone," Kim said. "Nobody in the house at all."

Dad was surprised. "That's right," Mom said. "We called and knocked, but there was no sign of anyone. I asked the people next door, but they said they didn't know where they were either, so we came straight home. The women all seem very busy today."

"Hmm," said Dad. " Probably Headman Tiger told him to leave the village after I showed him the poppy pictures. Well, well. The baby must have been better, Susan, or they wouldn't have gone," he comforted her. "Listen, I have an idea. Why don't we go cool off in the river; it's so hot, and we've all been rushing around."

"You go," Mom said. "I would like to have a nice cool drink and put my feet up inside the house. Bring the cats in; they can keep me company, and that way they won't follow you."

Sandee and Kim had a wonderful time splashing and swimming in the water, while Dad cooled off too and kept a look-out for danger. Once they thought they heard an elephant trumpeting, but it could have been one of the working elephants, it was too far off to be sure. Finally Dad called the girls to come out and, after getting toweled dry and changing into dry clothes, they carried their washed clothes home.

Mom was still resting when they arrived.

"Stay right there," Dad told her, "the girls and I will make supper."

Towards evening Headman Tiger came over to talk

with Malcolm about the tracking the village men had done. He said they had followed the tracks a long time, circling around, but had not found the elephants. "They've probably gone off to Burma by now," he said "and we'll never get them back from there."

"Do elephants travel very far when they have a young one?" Dad asked. "Wouldn't they stay in one area? After all, it's only two days since the girls took the picture; how far would a young elephant go? Maybe the helicopter frightened them and they are hiding."

"Maybe the elephant spirit does not want us to catch it. Maybe this is not a good thing to do," said Headman Tiger.

"But someone will catch it, or kill it; the forests are not so big anymore," Malcolm pointed out. "King Bhumibol would make sure it was well looked after—both of the elephants, together. Will you go out again at daylight, or will you wait for the soldiers to return?"

"Some of the men will go at daybreak. I will wait till the helicopter comes, to meet the elephant specialist." He got up. "I will go now," he said, and walked away.

The helicopter returned soon after daybreak, landing at the village, near the Green house. As the men were stepping out of the helicopter, Gleck came bursting out of the woods and rushed over to them to say that the elephants had been spotted. Two men were staying near them, but not too near, to watch where they were going, he said.

"Can you take us there? Is it very far?" the elephant specialist asked.

"I can take you." Gleck said. "But we will have to go quietly through the forest."

Headman Tiger came hurrying and said he would go too. The pilot stayed behind, but the other two men went with Gleck. Malcolm invited the pilot into the house to meet the rest of the family. Sandee and Kim, who had finished the dishes and other chores, asked if they could take a picture of the helicopter.

"I have a better idea," the pilot said. "You two get into it and I will take a picture of you, with your camera."

Mung and Dee and Granny Smiles came to see what was happening, and most of the other children came too, to see the helicopter. Granny Smiles went into the house to talk to Susan. She had brought the new Pwo Karen testament, wrapped in cloth, so Susan could read it with her. They sat down together in the big room, while the men stayed on the verandah.

Then the truck with soldiers returned. It stopped near the helicopter, sending the children running, but not very far. The soldiers went up onto the verandah too, to wait for the specialist to return and tell them what to do. Sandee went to help Mom bring cold drinks for everyone.

Around noon Gleck, Headman Tiger and the elephant specialist returned. Mrs. Tiger invited all of them to come to her house to eat. The village women had prepared a big meal of rice and spicy dishes. While the men were eating, they made plans for catching the elephants, which the other men were still guarding.

The plan was that the soldiers and village men would form a large half-circle some distance away from the elephants, so that the elephant-mother would not panic, and then they would slowly herd the elephants towards the road going through Striped Creek village. A big truck would be parked on the road, waiting for the elephants to arrive. Traffic would have to be stopped when the elephants neared the place. The inside of the truck would be camouflaged to make it look like a forest-cave. If necessary, a couple of working elephants would be brought to help too. The elephant-specialist was in charge of everything and would be staying as near to them as possible. Because they had found the elephants already some distance on the way towards the Striped Creek road, it was felt they could probably catch them the next day.

Right after lunch, the helicopter pilot flew out to pick up some newspaper and television reporters, but the specialist warned him not to fly over the area where the elephants were. "If they want pictures let them walk in like the rest of us," he said. "What's more important is that you make the arrangements for the truck and for additional men to be there at the road tomorrow morning. We don't know when we'll get there, but they had better be there when we do!"

After the helicopter left, the elephant-specialist, soldiers and Gleck, who was feeling very important now, trekked off into the forest again, taking food and camping gear with them. They planned to stay near the elephants all night.

Sandee helped Mom wash clothes and hang them up to dry. Kim was too excited to do anything except run from one thing to another. Dad firmly told her to sit down and write a letter to her grandparents, instead of wasting all her energy. Then, when she had just nicely got started, Mom said to Dad, "We'd better make sure the girls are wearing clean clothes, because the television reporter will want to interview them, since they were the ones who got all this started."

They had barely finished changing into their new dresses when the helicopter landed again and two reporters, one from the Bangkok TV station and the other from a newspaper, arrived. They took pictures of Sandee and Kim standing on the verandah of their house, and asked a lot of questions in Thai, which Dad helped the girls answer. Then, they took pictures of the village and asked for a guide to take them to the elephants.

Headman Tiger agreed to take them, but after he explained that he wasn't certain where they were now, because they were on the move, and it would take hours to find them, they decided to fly back to Hod with what they had, and come back next day to the road where the truck would be waiting. They did take pictures of the river where the white elephant was first seen, and of the forest around it. Dad and Kim went down with them to show them the elephant tracks.

Then Sandee came running down the path, shouting: "Dad, Dad, come quickly!"

"What is it, Sandee?" he asked, when she caught up with them. "What's wrong?"

"Hurry, it's Mom! She says the baby is coming!"

Immediately, Dad started running, followed by the girls and the reporters. When they got to the house, the helicopter pilot suggested to Dad that Mom fly out with them, to the hospital in Hod.

"There's enough room for her," he said. "We can leave right away; it would only take twenty minutes to get her to the hospital. You and the girls could follow in your

Rover. We don't have room for all of you."

Quickly, they helped Mom into the helicopter, with the suitcase she had packed a while earlier.

"We'll drive out too, as soon as we're packed and make arrangements for someone to look after the house," Dad told Mom. "Get someone to call our friends in Striped Creek, so they know you're there."

The girls waved as the helicopter lifted into the sky and soon was out of sight.

"Sandee, run to Granny Smiles and ask her to come here right away, please. Kim, you and I will pack some clothes and food to take."

Granny Smiles came over right away. She said she would look after the hens and cats and make sure no one broke into the house. Dad gave her a key to the house, because he was not sure how long they would be away. They got into the Rover.

"Oh wait, I forgot the camera!" Kim said, jumping out again. Granny let her into the house, then locked the door again, and watched them leave.

Chapter Ten

Two Babies

THE LAND-ROVER bumped along as fast as Dad could make it go, without damaging it, which wasn't very fast.

"Where will we stay, Dad?" Sandee wondered. "When will the baby be born; will we get there in time to see it?"

"The baby might be born already by the time we get there," Dad said. "I'm so thankful the helicopter was there. God provided before we even asked. We didn't expect the baby for two more weeks, or we would have left for the hospital sooner, but with the Christmas celebrations and the white elephant, we really couldn't leave anyway."

The girls kept quiet so Dad could concentrate on driving. Kim, who sat in the front, kept looking to see if there was any sign of the men herding the elephants, but there were too many hills and trees in the way.

"Dad," she asked, after a while, "will there be a television set where we stay in Hod?"

Dad laughed. "I have no idea, Kim. I'm not even sure where we'll stay. So you want to see yourself on television, do you? Well, we'll check it out. The helicopter pilot should be able to tell us about that."

Although the road was better after they passed the turn-off to Striped Creek village, it still took an hour to get to Hod. Dad drove straight to the hospital and parked. All three of them hurried into the hospital. A nurse told Dad to come with her, but Sandee and Kim had to sit in the waiting room. Everyone looked at them, and some people said things about them, noticing the Karen dresses they were still wearing. Then Dad came into the room, motioning the girls to come with him.

"You can come see Mom now—and your baby brother! He was born just before we got here."

Mom was lying in a clean bed, looking pale, but smiling. She was holding the baby, wrapped in a blanket. Sandee and Kim crowded up close to get a look at their brother.

"He's awfully small," Kim said, leaning up close, "but cute."

"What will we name him?" Sandee asked. "Have you decided already?"

"Not quite," Mom said. "And he isn't small; he's all of nine pounds! That's bigger than either of you were."

The nurse came in with a pot of tea and cookies. She took the baby and put him in a bassinet beside the bed. "Time for your mother to have a good sleep," she said. "You can see her again later."

Mom hugged them both and Dad took them out. He told them they would be staying at the nearby home of a Dutch couple who also worked for OMF. And, no, they did not have a television set, but they knew someone who did.

That evening there was another celebration—a small one, but still wonderful. Their friends cooked a delicious dinner, with ice-cream and chocolate sauce, sprinkled with peanuts, for dessert. When Dad asked the blessing on the food, he also thanked God for providing the helicopter to bring Mom to the hospital at exactly the right time to give birth to a fine, healthy baby.

Then, after dinner, they all walked to the hospital to say good-night to Mom, and returned home to get ready for bed themselves. But, before Sandee and Kim were asleep, Dad phoned the helicopter pilot to tell him about the baby boy.

"Would you and the girls like to fly with me tomorrow to see the elephants being loaded?" the pilot asked. "The truck will be going through here at night, ready for them whenever they arrive. I plan to fly down after an early breakfast."

"Yes! Yes!" shrieked the girls when they heard.

"Okay," Dad said. "But you must get right to sleep now. No talking." He closed the door to the little guest room which Sandee and Kim shared, and went back to exchange news about their work with their friends.

Sandee and Kim, who were sharing a double bed, lay very still for some time, trying to sleep. Then Kim whispered, very quietly, "I've thought of a name for our brother: Zachary Bee. Doesn't that sound nice?"

"You can't name our brother," Sandee said, "Mom and Dad will do that."

"But, don't you think it's a lovely name? Zachary Bee Green."

"I guess." Sandee said, doubtfully. "I guess it would be good to have a Karen name too. Anyway, we'd better sleep now. If you're not sleepy, try to remember everything good that's happened in our holiday, and I will too. Only the good things, remember."

They fell asleep so soundly that Dad had to come shake them awake for breakfast. Then they hurried to the helicopter to find the pilot and the TV cameraman packing their stuff, ready to take off. Quickly, Sandee and Kim were lifted in, and Dad found a place to sit too.

This was the girls' first ride in a helicopter, though of course, they had flown in airplanes before, all across oceans and countries. But this was different because they were not very high up, so they could see very clearly, upside down.

It took only a few minutes to get to the road on which the humongous truck was already parked. The helicopter landed on the road, some distance away from the truck, so that it wouldn't be noticeable. The TV cameraman got out to see what was happening, but the rest of them stayed in the helicopter. From where they were, they could easily see the fields and forest from which the elephants were expected to come.

Nothing seemed to be happening there yet, but, around the truck, soldiers were waiting; they had already placed trees and branches around the truck door, so that it did look like a forest-cave in which to hide. Sandee and Kim were allowed out for a quick look, but then hurried back to the helicopter, where they would be safe and out of the way.

Suddenly, they noticed movement in the bushes! Elephants! Three big ones could be seen slowly approaching! Two of them had a man sitting on top, guiding them along, but the third one did not. They were moving very slowly. After a bit they could also see people, in a large semi-circle, walking along. Sandee and Kim held their breath and waited to see if the baby elephant was all right.

"Here, Dad, you take the camera," Sandee said. "You are taller. Take a picture now, and then we can take more when they are closer."

Dad took a picture, pulled it out to be developed and handed the camera back to Sandee, so she could take the next one. Kim was hanging out the open door. The pilot was standing beside it. Everyone was very quiet; only the occasional elephant snort, and kind of a drumming noise made by the men, could be heard.

"There it is! There!" squealed Kim, pointing, "almost under it's mother. Quick, take a picture!"

"Sh—sh," Dad whispered. "Come back here, Kim."

Sandee handed him another picture to be developed and focussed the camera again. They could see the cameraman moving backwards, towards the truck, filming as he moved. The mother elephant stopped, waved her trunk around, bent down to touch and nuzzle her young one, and then—quietly urged forward by the men on the backs of the other elephants, started walking again. The men all moved in closer now, still making the drumming noise.

"There's Gleck," whispered Sandee, taking another picture, "and Headman Tiger."

They could see the elephant-specialist moving up closer to the mother and calf—and then everyone moved right in, nearly pushing the baby elephant up the ramp, with the mother going right in too! Sandee and Kim couldn't see what happened after that, but soon the truck motor started and the truck moved away, very slowly and carefully. The elephant specialist was in the cab of the truck, along with the driver and another man.

Kim started to cry. Dad picked her up onto his lap to hug her. "The king will see to it that they get very good care, Kimberly Ann; they will be safer and happier there than in forests where hunters would soon be after them. And the elephant specialist is in the truck too; he'll make sure they get the best of care. We'll go to see them in Bangkok on your next holiday."

The pilot and cameraman returned to the helicopter, ready for the lift-off. In a few minutes, they landed in Hod again.

"Now let's go see Mom," Dad said.

"And Zachary Bee," Kim and Sandee added.

Dad looked puzzled. "Who's Zachary Bee?"

"Our brother," they said together, laughing. "We named him last night!"